To Oscar, Conrad and Caspar
with all my love
**A.M.**

For my super nephews Tom and Euan
and my big brother Matt
**A.T.S.**

First published in 2010
by Meadowside Children's Books
185 Fleet Street, London EC4A 2HS
www.meadowsidebooks.com

Text © Anna Maxted 2010
Illustrations © Alex T. Smith 2010

# Tom & Matt

# THE

# BADDIE

Written by
**ANNA MAXTED**

Illustrated by
**ALEX T. SMITH**

meadowside
CHILDREN'S BOOKS

YOU ARE HERE

# CONTENTS

DEEP SPACE

# 1. THE BIGGEST PAIR OF VILLAINS ON THE PLANET

"You are the biggest pair of villains on the planet," said Daddy. "Now hand over your weapons!"

"No way," said Tom. "I need this sword."

"No way," said Matt. "This is my best ever blaster."

Mummy was out, and Daddy was in charge. The Baby was eating dirt off the floor. And Tom and Matt were fighting.

Tom was a superhero, **FIRE RAIDER**. He wore a mask and a cape with a **T** on it. Matt was **NA-NA-NER**, a pink alien. Matt was only three and thought he was a girl. He was dressed in his pants. He didn't like other clothes.

7

# TOM & MATT

Daddy

"Give me the sword and the blaster," said Daddy. "Before someone loses an eye!"

"No," said Tom. "You stink!"

"Yeah," said Matt. "You stink!"

"Nonsense," said Daddy, as loud as a cross rhinoceros. "I had a shower this morning. I'm as clean as a whistle."

Tom and Matt carried on fighting.

**"RIGHT!"** shouted Daddy. "The sword and the blaster are going on top of the fridge. And there will be none of your TV for a week. Superheroes are banned from the house. From now on, we watch only the news and cooking programmes. And in seven days, I shall test you on current events then make you cook me a soufflé! Matt! Give me that sword or you're going to Bin Man School."

# THE BADDIE

Bin Man School was a made-up thing that Daddy said to scare Matt when Matt was very bad.

"What's Bin Man School, Daddy?" said Tom, even though he knew. He just liked to scare his little brother.

"Bin Man School is an Academy of the Science of Rubbish Removal. It lasts for twelve years, and returns children to their parents fully grown!"

"I don't want to go to Bin Man School!" wailed Matt.

"Then," roared Daddy, as red in the face as a jam doughnut, "act like a good boy instead of a banana-brain!"

"And you!" Daddy pointed at Tom. "Don't whack your brother on the head with a sword! Or I'll put you on Pooh Patrol!"

Pooh Patrol was another made-up thing that Daddy said to scare Tom. It was a field full of dog pooh that you had to tidy up with your bare hands.

# THE BADDIE

Actually, Mummy had told Daddy that he was not allowed to scare Tom and Matt with Bin Man School or Pooh Patrol. But Mummy was out. And Daddy was in charge. And Tom and Matt were fighting.

"Sorry Daddy."

"Sorry Daddy."

"It's nearly bed time, thank goodness," said Daddy. "I'm going upstairs to run you a bath. Try not to be evil for five seconds!"

While Daddy ran the bath, Matt waggled his bottom backwards and forwards at Tom and started shouting, **"MY BOTTOM, MY WILL-"**

Tom grabbed his sword and clonked Matt on the head.

Matt screeched like a pirate's parrot, and bit Tom on the arm.

# TOM & MATT

"**OWWWWWWW!**" roared Tom.

Daddy thumped down the stairs and shouted, "That's IT! Get up here, now! Get in the bath! Are all children this bad or is it just you two?"

Tom and Matt got in the bath. They played nicely for one minute. Then they had a water fight.

When they were in bed, Tom said, "I don't want to go to sleep. I'm bored. I want to play."

# THE BADDIE

"Me too," said Matt.

"Shall we go in the Hide Out?"

"Yes! Tom, you are a genius!"

The Hide Out was a top-secret den, in Matt and Tom's room. It was the strongest fortress in the universe. Tom and Matt had made it from chairs and sheets and blankets. If you went inside, it made you **INVISIBLE**.

the Hideout

KEEP OUT.

Their best game was to dress as superheroes, and creep into the Hide Out. They always took a torch, a blaster, biscuits, and all the other supplies that a modern superhero needs. And then they would sit in the Hide Out, and prepare for battle.

Tom jumped out of bed and grabbed his torch.

Just then, he heard a noise.

It was a 'clank'. It sounded like metal banging on metal.

There it was again.

**'CLINK! CLANK!'**

What was it?

Who was it?

"What's that noise?" said Matt. "I'm scared."

The noise was coming from inside the Hide Out.

# 2.
# 3 SUPERHEROES

**"SHHH!"** said Tom.

Tom was rubbish at being quiet. And Matt was a big-bin-lorry-full-of-rubbish at being quiet.

But now, neither boy made even the tiniest noise.

It was very dark in the room, but Tom was too scared to turn on his torch. Slowly, Tom picked up his Light Saver and crept towards the Hide Out. Matt pulled the duvet up to his nose.

And then, Tom trod on Rory Dragon.

Rory Dragon was a big toy dragon. If you pressed a button, his eyes flashed red and he gave a loud roar. Rory Dragon was very good at scaring the Baby away from their toys.

**"ROAAARRR!"** said Rory Dragon.

A zip of blue light illuminated the room. Rory Dragon went **'ROAR-BANG!'** and in a big flash of yellow light and a puff of white smoke, he was gone.

Matt squealed and hid under the duvet.

Tom dropped his Light Saver and opened his mouth to yell, **"DADDEEEEE!"**

But no sound came out. It was like a bad

dream. He couldn't move. He couldn't speak.

The Hide Out glowed with a spooky blue light. There was a **'CLANK!'** and a rush of cold wind. And right in front of Tom lines appeared in the air. It was like a drawing of a robot being slowly coloured in. **'WHIRR! CLONK!'** Tom's eyes nearly popped out of his head. He felt the hair stand up on the back of his neck.

It was a creature in silver body armour. He had the body of a man. But his helmet was shaped like a dog's head. A small row of green and red lights beeped and flickered on the front of his suit. And he was carrying the biggest space blaster that Tom had ever seen.

# TOM & MATT

He lifted both hands and Tom closed his eyes. Was he going to be zapped like Rory Dragon? After a second, he opened his eyes. The creature had only lifted his hands to take off his helmet.

Oh! He was a man. Not a dog.

He had black messy hair. And his eyes were purple. He spoke in a deep voice. It sounded as if his vocal chords were made of metal. So he wasn't a man... **HE WAS AN ALIEN**.

# 3. THE CAT PAN

"Greetings, Tom and Matt. I come from the Planet Dog Star. My name is the Captain–OW!"

**'DONK!'** A football bounced off the Captain's head.

**"HA-HA HA-HA-HA!"**

Tom and the Captain turned to see Matt jumping on the bed. "Got you, got you! You can't get me!"

"Matt!" hissed Tom. He could speak again! "Stop it! Don't hurt him, Captain! He's only three!"

The Captain's eyes glowed. He took a step closer to Matt. Slowly, so the Captain didn't see, Tom felt for his Light Saver. But as soon as he found it, he dropped it with a gasp. It was red hot.

Now, Matt was chanting, **"OO-OO-OO!"** jumping up and down, and pretending to be an ape.

"Matthew!" said the Captain, "you are not allowed to play football in the house! You've been told a hundred times! Stop jumping! You'll ruin the mattress!"

Matt stopped jumping. He frowned. "Mummy?" he said. "Is that you? Are you in a wig?"

"Mummy?!" shouted the Captain in a great dinosaur roar. "Do I look like Mummy? Am I wearing a dress?"

"No!" said Tom and Matt.

The Captain waved a silver glove. It left a trail of silver sparkles in the air.

"Cool," said Tom.

The Captain smiled. "I am a superhero from

the Planet Dog Star.
It is in a far
off galaxy,
twenty million
miles beyond the
moon. Do a sharp left at
the black hole, carry on
for five light years – over the
falling stars – and there it
is. You can't miss it."

← BLACK HOLE

"Wow," said Tom.

"Cool, man," said Matt.

"I know," said the Captain, "I am very cool."
He smiled. "But I have to thank you boys. You
saved my life."

"How?" said Tom.

The man pointed to the chairs
covered in sheets and blankets.

"You built the Hide Out." He
dropped his voice to a whisper. "The strongest
fortress in the galaxy. I have been hiding in it
from my arch enemy for six days."

"Six days!" said Tom.

"Liar, liar, pants on fire!" said Matt.

The Captain checked his pants. "Negative," he said. "Pants not on fire."

"But... if you were in the Hide Out all this time, why didn't we see you?" said Tom.

The Captain gave Tom an odd look. "It made me invisible of course!"

"But," said Tom, "that's only pretend!"

"Don't be silly," said the Captain. He smiled. He had nice white teeth. "Try it."

Slowly, Tom and Matt crawled into the Hide Out. And it was true. When Tom looked down at himself, all he saw was air. Matt was also invisible and his feet banged on the floor as he jumped up and down shouting, "Look at me! Look at me!"

Tom scrambled out. It was amazing to be invisible, but it was even more amazing to have a superhero in your bedroom.

"Captain," said Tom, nervously. "Who is your arch enemy?"

The Captain made a rude face. **"JONNY SUPERSONIC."**

Tom gasped. "Is he very evil?"

The Captain gave a loud snort. "Tell me, Tom. Who is your arch enemy?"

"My cousin, Horace," said Tom. "He's so mean. He always wants to win at football, and at everything. And he says my bike is rubbish. And he punches. And he never lets Matt join in."

"Mm," said the Captain. "Well, Jonny Supersonic is like Horace, but a trillion million times worse. His punch is supersonic! It can knock you through a wall! Oh, he thinks he's so great! Jonny Supersonic wants to crush me like an ant! He wants to zap me! He wants to frazzle me to a burnt crisp!"

24

# THE BADDIE

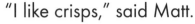

"I like crisps," said Matt.

"Captain," said Tom. "Do you have powers?"

**"ONLY ABOUT A THOUSAND! I CAN FLY, I CAN–"**

"Cat Pan! Cat Pan!" said Matt. "I have powers! I can fly!"

"What? No you can't! And don't call me Cat Pan. 'Captain' means 'in charge'. 'Cat Pan' means 'a cat's toilet'!"

"I can fly!" said Matt. "Look!" And he jumped off the bed. **"WHOOSH!"**

"That's not flying! You just made a noise with your mouth!"

"Captain," said Tom, before Matt started a fight with a superhero. "Can we help you beat Jonny Supersonic?"

The Captain smiled. "Well thank you for asking, Tom. Yes, you can."

# 4
## PREPARE FOR BLAST OFF!!!

The next day, Mummy came in. She looked at the Hide Out and said, "That sheet is filthy! I'm going to wash it."

Before they could stop her, she'd whipped off the roof.

KEEP OUT!

"Stop!" shouted Tom. But it was too late. Without the roof to protect him, the Captain would no longer be invisible! Tom waited for Mummy to see him and shout, "Help! Police!"

**"OOH,"** said Mummy, bending down. "I don't remember this one. Is this a new toy?"

Tom looked. Mummy was holding what looked like a toy model of the Captain.

He had shrunk himself! His powers were so cool!

"Is it one of those stretchy toys?" said Mummy, giving the Captain's arm a yank.

**"OW!"**

"It's one of those talking toys!" said Mummy. "What else does it say?" she said, giving the Captain a big hard jab in the belly.

**"GET OFF!"**

# TOM & MATT

"I wish you boys would tidy up," said Mummy. And before Tom could stop her, she dropped the Captain into the toy box.

**"DOUBLE OW! THAT HURT!"**

"I don't like that toy," said Mummy. "It's got a funny head."

Tom snatched up the Captain and whispered, "Sorry!" The Captain glared.

"Now," said Mummy. "I'm going to the shop to buy tea, fish and toilet paper. I'm so excited. I beg you to be good for Daddy. Kiss kiss!"

As soon as Mummy shut the door, the Captain grew back to his full size.

Tom and Matt gazed up at him.

# THE BADDIE

He looked very big and powerful. His silver suit glinted in the light. His dog head helmet made him look regal – like a king or a god from Ancient Egypt.

He held his blaster as if ready to fire.

"Captain!" said Tom. "Can we go now? We want to go to the Planet Dog Star now! Please take us with you!"

"Please, Cat Pan!" said Matt. "Please please please!"

The Captain nodded.

"Alright, boys, but we must hurry!" he said. "I need you to get dressed in your best superhero outfits! Now! Find your swords and your blasters and your light savers! We are flying into space to find Jonny Supersonic and crush him for good!"

"Hooray!" shouted Tom and Matt.

"I love you," added Matt. "You're the best Cat Pan in the world!"

"Go!" said the Captain.

Tom and Matt got dressed so fast Mummy and Daddy would have fallen flat on their faces in shock. When Mummy and Daddy told Tom and Matt to get dressed, Tom and Matt were as slow as snails. But when a superhero tells you to get dressed – you obey!

This is very unfair to Mummies and Daddies. But never mind!

Tom was wearing his own superhero outfit. He wore his best blue top with gold stars on it. He wore his camouflage shorts. And he wore his trainers with flashing lights.

Matt wore a cape, and spotty pants and his green swimming goggles.

"Perfect!" said the Captain. "Now take me to your spaceship!"

# 5. The Best Spaceship in the Galaxy

Tom's mouth fell open. "But..." he said. "But we don't have a spaceship. Where is your spaceship?"

"It's parked at the end of the garden," said the Captain, "in the flower bed. It has purple stripes and a green control panel. It is streak-of-light fast. But we can't use it. If we do, Jonny Supersonic will find us and zap us! We need to fly under cover. We have to go in disguise!"

# THE BADDIE

"I see the moon and the moon sees me!" sang Matt.

"But..." said Tom.

"But nothing!" said the Captain. "I've seen your spaceship! I can't wait to fly it! It's state of the art! You designed the control panel, Tom. And Matt made the fuel jets. Your spaceship is the envy of the galaxy!"

Tom wasn't sure he understood. "You mean... the spaceship in the hall? But that's not a spaceship... it's a box! It's made of cardboard!"

The Captain looked at Tom as if he was bonkers crazy. "Yes," he said. "What else should it be made of? Metal? Ha ha ha! It would fall to bits!"

"It's a really good spaceship," said Matt. "I did it with glue." He put on a deep growly voice. "Come on! Let's go to space!"

Tom frowned. No one could fly to space in a box! But then, the Captain did have special powers. "Yes!" he shouted. "Jonny Supersonic, prepare to be bank-quished! Planet Dog Star here we come!"

He jumped into the box. So did Matt. "I'll drive," said the Captain. "I know the way. Seat belts on! Prepare for take off!"

There was a jolt, and a vroom! And the box shot up in the air – almost to the ceiling.

"Wow!" shouted Tom. **"OH, WOW!"**

"I'm hungry," said Matt. "I need to do a wee."

The box dropped to the floor. 'Bonk!'

Two minutes later, the box took off again. Or rather the spaceship took off again. It was the prized THIS WAY UP model. On board were three brave superheroes –

the Captain, Tom, and Matt. There was also food for the mission: a packet of pig sweets, pink yoghurt with no bits, apple juice, stick bread, holey cheese, milk, and chocolate cereal.

Up, up, and up they flew, high above the houses and trees. Everything looked so little. Tom felt like a giant.

The Captain was right. This was a great spaceship. Like magic, the box had grown... It was huge. And it was warm and snug. There was a cube-shaped roof of super-strong glass.

# TOM & MATT

Tom's control panel – with a dial drawn on in red, yellow, and blue felt tip – beeped happily.

"**WOOOOO HOO!**" shouted the Captain. "This baby drives itself!"

"It's not a baby," said Matt. "It's a spaceship, silly!"

Tom lifted his head and gazed up at the glass roof. The sky was dark, and lit with stars. And there, like a big yellow cut of cheese, hung...

"**THE MOON!**" yelled Tom. "Look Matt! It's so close!"

"The moon!" yelled Matt. "The moon is a balloon!"

"The moon!" yelled the Captain. "We're on our way!"

# 6. Space Fight!

"Are we there yet?" said Matt.

"Nearly," said the Captain.

"I feel sick," said Matt.

"Drink some water," said the Captain.

"I need to do another wee," said Matt.

"Hold it in," said the Captain.

"Where's Mummy?" said Matt.

**"SILENCE,"** said the Captain, **"OR I'LL HAVE AN ACCIDENT!"**

"Mummy is at home," said Tom. "You'll see her soon. We are superheroes now. The Captain needs our help!"

Tom didn't want Matt to cry and sulk in the middle of a mission.

In true life, Tom was a bit worried. If he went on his bike to the park, Mummy shouted, 'Tom! Not so fast! Stay close!'

Now, he was ten million light years away from Mummy. That wasn't close.

But... they were superheroes! They had blasters and swords and light savers. They also had a balloon pump and Mummy's metal whisk for making burnt cakes and her pasta scoop. Tom and Matt were not allowed to play with the metal whisk or the pasta scoop but this was important.

not allowed (at all!)

Mummy would not be cross if she knew they were fighting a baddie.

But, Tom knew that Mummy did not like fighting. And she liked her boys to stay close.

"Don't be sad," said the Captain. "If you want, we can go and get your Mummy and your Daddy!"

"Yes!" said Tom.

Matt said nothing. He was not talking to the Cat Pan because the Cat Pan had shouted.

"Matt?" said the Captain. "Shall we get Mummy?"

Matt made a cross face. **"DON'T SHOUT AT ME! YOU DONK-HEAD! YOU HURT MY FEELINGS!"**

He ran at the Captain and kicked his ankle.

**"OW!"** said the Captain.

"Matt!" said Tom. "Say sorry!"

Tom didn't want the Captain to get cross. Even goodies were scary when they got cross.

**"NO,"** said Matt.

The Captain's eyes glowed purple. But as he turned to Matt, there was a massive jolt. The spaceship lurched.

Tom and Matt and the Captain all fell over in a big pile.

"What was that?" yelled Tom. He had Matt's foot in his face.

"I'm scared!" yelled Matt. He had Tom's knee in his neck.

"We're under fire!" yelled the Captain. He had Matt's bottom on his head. "Get off!"

"I just did a pop-off on your head," said Matt. "I am Fart Guy!"

**'POW POW! POW POW!'**

"It's Jonny Supersonic!" shouted the Captain. "He's going to gloop the whole ship!"

There in the dark of space, Tom saw a huge spaceship, painted silver. It was zooming straight at them. It was firing big green balls

of what looked like jelly. Inside the ship, Tom could just see someone in a red suit and a silver helmet. The Baddie!

Tom ran to the back of the ship and got his light saver. The ship was wobbling and he banged his head. But Tom was very brave. He got the sword for Matt and the metal whisk.

"Don't be scared Matt," he said. "I'll keep you safe."

Sometimes Tom hated Matt, but really he loved him. Tom was a good big brother.

The Captain ran to the controls, and pressed 'FIRE'.

**'NEOOW! NEOOW!'**

"Bother! Missed! The gun barrels must be wonky."

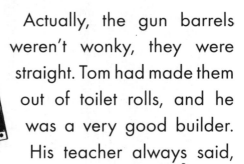

Actually, the gun barrels weren't wonky, they were straight. Tom had made them out of toilet rolls, and he was a very good builder. His teacher always said, *"Everyone is good at something."* And Tom was good at building.

**'POW POW! POW POW!'**

The ship kept wobbling. Tom was scared.

"We must retreat!" shouted the Captain. "He's too powerful! I say we head for the Dark Side of the Moon! He'll never find us there!"

"I know what to do!" said Matt. "Press the **NEE-NAW BUTTON**!"

"What the monkey gibbon is a **NEE-NAW BUTTON**?" said the Captain.

"It's that," said Matt.

And he smacked down his hand on a big black scribble on the control panel. Tom remembered him doing it. Tom had just finished the control panel. And Matt had come over with a black felt tip, and ruined it.

'**WOOOSH!**'

They went down, fast, and their tummies went up, like in a lift.

"Help!" shouted the Captain.

There was a thump, and silence. And they were back in Tom and Matt's house, on the landing, in a box.

"**WOW!**" said the Captain.

"Matt!" said Tom. "You're a genius! You drew an emergency button!"

"Yes," said Matt. "A **NEE-NAW BUTTON**."

He jumped out of the ship and shouted, "Mummy! I'm home!"

"Hello, darling!" shouted Mummy from downstairs. "Daddy says you've been as good as gold!"

"We went to space!" shouted Matt. "We need back-up! Get Daddy!"

The Captain gave Tom a poke in the arm. "Get Daddy!"

So Tom ran, with Matt, to get Mummy and Daddy. Tom dragged Daddy off the computer, and Matt held Mummy's hand.

"Come and see our spaceship," said Tom.

He knew that Mummy wouldn't think it was a real spaceship, until it was up in the air.

"Get in!" said Matt, showing Mummy the spaceship. Then he sang, "Three little men in

a flying saucer came down to earth one day!"
Matt did like singing.

**"OOH,"** said Mummy, as she stepped into
the box. "This is fun!"

"Are we going to fight the baddie?" said
Daddy. "It's a bit of a squash in here."

"It gets bigger!" said Matt.

Tom saw that the Captain had shrunk to the
size of a toy. He was lying on the floor of the
box. Tom picked him up.

"Put me back in the ship," hissed
the Captain. "You and Matt –
go and get supplies!"

Tom did as he was told and
put the Captain in the ship
with Mummy and Daddy.
Then he went downstairs
with Matt to get supplies.

"Mummy and Daddy
– stay there!" he shouted.
"We need to get supplies!"

"Nothing sharp please!"
said Mummy.

# TOM & MATT

Tom and Matt got more pig sweets. And Matt got the wooden spoon. And Tom got their toy handcuffs. And Matt took off his green swimming goggles and put on his pink sunglasses.

Then they ran back upstairs.

"Mummy! Daddy! We're back!"

But the landing was deserted.

# THE BADDIE

There was no box. There was no Captain. There was no Mummy. And there was no Daddy. They were gone.

"Where's Mummy?" said Matt, dropping the wooden spoon. "Where's Daddy?"

"I don't know," said Tom.

He felt scared suddenly.

Matt clung to Tom and started to cry.

# 7.

# JONNY SUPERSONIC

There was a flash of green lightning, and the house shook like a jelly on a plate. A thick cloud of green smoke filled the air, and for a second, Tom thought the house was on fire. But the smoke smelled nice – like sausages.

"Matt!" shouted Tom. "Mummy and Daddy and the Captain are back!"

"Hooray!" shouted Matt.

They jumped up and down. Slowly the smoke cleared, and a big boy – at least ten – stood before them. He had two laser blasters on his belt. He had a cross face. He wore a shiny red suit, and a silver helmet.

There were a few crumbs around his mouth as if he had just eaten a biscuit.

Tom gasped. It was the Baddie! It was Jonny Supersonic! In his house.

Tom's house was his best place. He loved the soft old sofa where he cuddled up with Mummy and Daddy, and rolled around with Matt. Tom loved his room where he arranged all his soldiers and dreamed of aliens on a motorbike flying past the moon. Tom loved his bed, where the cat, heavy and warm, slept on his legs at night. Tom loved the kitchen, which smelled of dinner and where there were interesting things in the drawers. Tom loved the black and white tiles on the hallway floor, and the loose one, which he took out and put back in, like a puzzle.

It was a small, scruffy house but Tom loved it because it contained his favourite people and it made him feel safe. But now a baddie was in his house and it felt very wrong.

Jonny Supersonic took off his helmet.

"So," he said, in a mean voice, "Tom and Matt – or should I say – **FIRE RAIDER** and **FART GUY**. We meet at last!"

Matt picked up the wooden spoon and hit Jonny Supersonic on the knee. **"FART GUY!"** he shouted, one fist in the air. "Yes!"

**"FIRE RAIDER!"** yelled Tom, and shone his torch in Jonny's eyes. Jonny put up his hand to block the light – and Matt hit him with the wooden spoon on the other knee.

## THE BADDIE

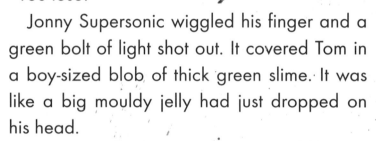

"**HI-YA!**" they shouted together and did their best karate chops.

"Boom chaka chaka boom!" added Matt. "You lose!"

Jonny Supersonic wiggled his finger and a green bolt of light shot out. It covered Tom in a boy-sized blob of thick green slime. It was like a big mouldy jelly had just dropped on his head.

"**BLUB!**" shouted Matt, who was also covered in green slime. "I'm trapped! In a giant booger! Disgusting! Blow your nose in a tissue!"

"Yeah, **BOOGER BOY**!" shouted Tom. "Let us go!"

"Oh certainly!" said Jonny. But he didn't. Tom felt himself lifted into the air inside the slime ball.

"Hey!" cried Tom. "This thing stinks!"

"Stop!" yelled Matt. "I'm a superhero! I am Fart Guy!"

Jonny Supersonic laughed. "You're not a superhero, Fart Guy. You're a stupid-hero!"

Jonny Supersonic did a loud burp, and suddenly Tom and Matt were no longer in their house.

They were inside the large silver spaceship.

# THE BADDIE

It had portholes all along the sides, and big computers with blinking lights. There was a muddy silver suit lying on the floor, and a pair of green pants, and some crumpled socks. There were sweet wrappers scrunched up near the bin, and the walls were covered with thousands of football stickers – they seemed to be from planets all over the universe.

Oh no. It was Jonny's spaceship.

"Where are you taking us?" shouted Tom. "You'll be sorry when Daddy finds out!"

Tom had to try and scare Jonny and make him stop. What else could he do? They weren't superheroes. They didn't have powers. They were just two boys with plastic swords. And this baddie was taking them to another planet far, far away.

# 8. WHAT A SLIME BALL (yuck!)

Jonny sat on a big silver seat in front of the controls, while Tom and Matt dangled in mid-air inside their slime balls. Tom had slime in his ears and slime up his nose. He had slime up his jumper and slime down his trousers. And he felt like he was wearing slime glasses. Slime glasses are not like sunglasses. They make everything look blurred and green.

Then a robotic voice started a count down. "FIVE, FOUR, THREE, TWO, ONE AND A HALF, ONE AND A QUARTER, ONE – COMING, READY OR NOT! – I MEAN, BLAST OFF!"

The spaceship shot into the air, fast as the speed of light, and inside their green gloop,

Tom and Matt were bounced up and down like rubber balls.

"My Daddy is going to put you on **POOH PATROL**!" shouted Tom.

"My Mummy will tell you off!" shouted Matt. "She will put you on the Naughty Step for **A MILLION YEARS**!"

"Oh, really?" said Jonny Supersonic, as Matt bounced past him upside down. "Fart Guy – where you are going, you won't be seeing this Mummy person for a million years!"

Tom was scared. He wanted to cry but he refused.

Matt didn't refuse. He cried and screamed and wailed and yowled and bawled and roared and screeched – on and on and on and on like a howler monkey with a headache.

"Stop it!" shouted Jonny Supersonic. "My ears are going to burst!"

**"WAAAAAAAAAAAAAAAAAAAAAAAAA AAAAAAAAAH!"**

"Stop it!" shouted Jonny Supersonic. "My head is going to explode!"

# THE BADDIE

"WAAAAAAAAAAAAAAAAAAAAAAAA
AAAAAAAAAH!"

"Stop it!" shouted Jonny Supersonic. "Or I'll zap you!"

"WAAAAAAAAAAAAAAAAAAAAAAAA
AAAAAAAAAH!"

"It won't work," said Tom, from inside his slime. "He won't stop crying. You have to give him a sweet."

"But that's bribery!" said Jonny Supersonic. "I'm not rewarding him for acting like a chimpanzee!"

"WAAAAAAAAAAAAAAAAAAAAAAAA
AAAAAAAAAAAAAAAAAAAAAAAAH!"

## TOM & MATT

Jonny Supersonic dug in his pocket so fast his fingers were a blur. He pulled out a sweet. He clapped his hands. The gloop went splat! Tom and Matt fell to the floor, still slimy, but free. Jonny gave Matt the sweet. Matt stopped crying. "Fank you," he said.

Jonny glared at Tom. "Don't tell anyone," he said.

Tom scraped some gloop out of his ear with his finger. It was great to be out of the slime ball. Now he could see outside. He could see space. It wasn't at all like in the books, but maybe the people who had written the books hadn't been out this far.

There were purple wisps of cloud, and pink stars, and Tom saw a teddy bear in a space helmet fly past in a picnic basket.

## THE BADDIE

"Hello, Bear in the Air!" said Jonny, and waved.

Bear in the Air waved back.

"SIT! FASTEN SEATBELTS! DON'T KICK THE SEAT IN FRONT!" shouted the robotic voice. "PREPARE FOR LANDING!"

Then Jonny Supersonic hit the brake, and the spaceship started to fall through the air like a brick.

Tom and Matt yelled – but just before they hit the ground the ship slowed – and landed as softly as a feather falling into a nest.

"WELCOME TO THE PLANET DOG STAR!" said the robotic voice. "PREPARE TO DISEMBARK. THAT MEANS 'GET OFF'."

# 9

## The Prison at the
# EDGE
### of the
# UNIVERSE

"Where are we?" said Tom.

"I want to go home," said Matt.

They were inside a big gloomy building. Water dripped from the ceiling, and the room smelt like cat food and old fish. There were no windows and as soon as they stepped through it, the door vanished. It was dark – the only light was a glowing ball on a desk that buzzed, as if there was a fly trapped inside.

Tom heard a rustling sound, and froze. He squinted, into the dimness, and jumped in fright. At the end of the room there was a row of jail cells. They all had thick cardboard bars across the front, and there were people – or things – inside them.

He held Matt's hand tightly, and peered closer.

Then Tom made a small squeak – he couldn't help it. Inside those cells were monsters.

His eyes were used to the dark now, and he could see a spider, the size of Daddy. Its thick black hairy legs were creeping between the bars, reaching, feeling towards him.

Even though Mummy said that spiders were harmless, she screeched if she saw one in the bath, so Tom was scared of spiders too.

Tom was scared of baby spiders so little they still wore nappies.

He hardly dared look in the next cell, but he did. Inside was a dark red stringy alien – it had no skin. Its insides were all outside. Tom felt like he might be sick.

Just then, he heard heavy footsteps. They were coming closer, thud, thud, thud.

Tom squeezed Matt's hand.

# THE BADDIE

A door burst open, and a great big fat man, in a tight blue uniform, with a blaster tucked into his belt, waddled in. "Sorry to keep you waiting, Mr Supersonic," he boomed. "The builders digging the bottomless pit are taking forever."

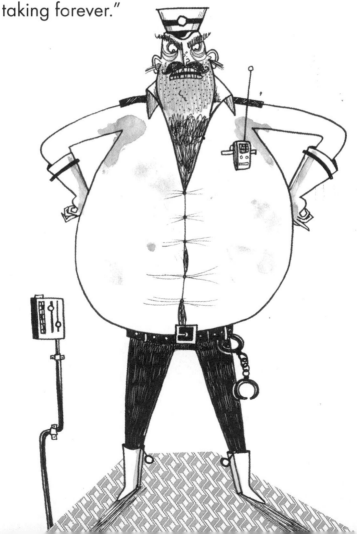

He crouched down until his face was level with Tom and Matt. He had very hairy nostrils. He needed to clean his teeth. "So!" he bellowed. "Who do we have here?"

Matt twisted his head away and folded his arms. Tom pressed his lips together.

Jonny Supersonic answered. "Fire Raider and Fart Guy!"

The big fat man jumped back. Tom could hear scared voices from the cells. When he dared look, he saw that the huge spider had folded into itself like an umbrella. The red alien had backed into a corner of his cell.

"Settle down, Tarantula Boy and Scarlet Bogey!" roared the big fat man. "They can't get you!"

# THE BADDIE

He spoke into his radio. "This is the Chief of Police, requesting urgent back up. Officer Bolognese, back away from the chocolate biscuits, and get to the front desk. Mr Supersonic has arrested the biggest villains on Planet Earth – Fire Raider and Fart Guy – this station is on red alert. Repeat, the super baddies, Fire Raider and Fart Guy have been brought in!"

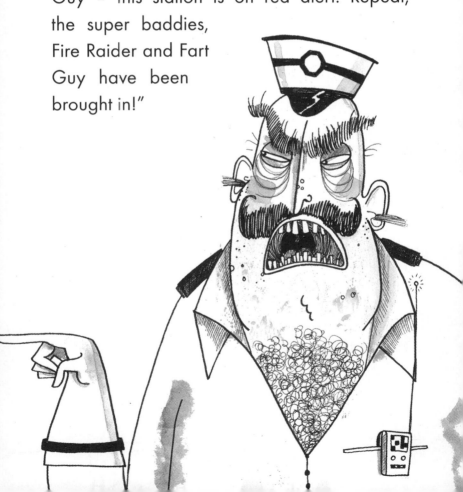

# 10. Goodies and BADDIES and BADDIES and Goodies

"Hey!" shouted Tom. "We're not baddies. We're goodies!"

"Hay is for horses," said the Chief of Police, and he picked up Tom and Matt and plonked them in a cell.

Then he turned away. "Thank you, Mr Supersonic. You really are the best super hero ever. Now if only you could catch the evil Captain, we'd all sleep easier at night. I'm hardly getting a wink of sleep – my Jonny Supersonic Night Light is out of batteries."

Tom stared at Jonny Supersonic. What! Was he a goody? And why was the Chief of Police calling the Captain evil?

"Jonny Supersonic!" he shouted. "We are goodies!"

The Chief of Police turned back to Tom and Matt. "Right," he said. "We have rules here. So listen up!"

**RULE ONE:** If you run in your cell, you stand on one leg for the rest of the week.

**RULE TWO:** If you talk, you get your mouth washed out with purple soap.

**RULE THREE:** All food must be eaten. The menu today is: goat milk and blue cheese for breakfast. Lunch is cabbage, sprouts and asparagus. Supper is some kind of brown goo mixed into a gunge. It will be the same tomorrow, and for the next million years after that.

"We are goodies!" shouted Tom.
"Stand on one leg!"

**"WE ARE NOT NAUGHTY!"** shouted Matt. **"WE ARE GOODIES!"**

Matt's voice was so loud, the glass light ball shattered, and the room was plunged into darkness.

Tom switched on his torch.

The Chief of Police and Jonny Supersonic stared at the boys. Then they looked at each other and shook their heads.

"We are goodies!" said Tom. "I promise."

The Chief of Police frowned. "You promise?" he said. "Then it must be true!"

Jonny Supersonic shook his head. "But the man they call 'Daddy' said they were the biggest villains on Earth!"

"Yes!" said the Chief of Police. "And they had Captain Chaos over for a play date. He is the biggest, meanest, wickedest super-villain on the Planet Dog Star!"

Tom shook the bars of his cell and tore one by accident.

The Chief of Police stared. "He can rip cardboard!" he said. He pulled out his blaster.

Jonny nodded. "Their powers are amazing. You should see the spaceship they built. And Fart Guy's pop-offs could blow your head off."

"Stop!" said Tom. "Please listen! Daddy was joking. And we didn't know the Captain was a baddie! The Captain came to us!"

"Yes!" said Jonny Supersonic. "You see, the Captain thought you were super villains too. He thought you would help him with his evil plan."

"The Cat Pan is a donk head," said Matt. "He zapped Rory Dragon. And he shouted at me. That is **NOT COOL**."

Tom bent the other cardboard bars and climbed out of the cell. Matt followed.

"I'm so sorry for the mistake!" said the Chief of Police. "If we had known that you were super heroes..." He glared at Jonny Supersonic.

"Even goodies get it wrong sometimes," said Jonny.

Tom was shocked that the **GOODIES** had thought he and Matt were **BADDIES**. Tom and Matt never meant to be bad. Not even that time when they'd used all Mummy's green 'Clowns Shower Gel' to make a poisonous potion.

"You **GLOOPED** us," said Tom, to Jonny Supersonic.

Jonny Supersonic stared at the ground. "I apologise," he said gruffly to Tom and Matt. "I only gloop **BADDIES** and I thought you were baddies. It was my fault. I would like to blame it on you, but I won't."

The Chief of Police saluted Jonny. "That's very big of you, Supersonic!"

Jonny Supersonic blushed.

"Now," said the Chief of Police. "Can I get you gentlemen something to eat and drink? My treat! Feel free to order **TWO**

**DESSERTS!** We have a delightful cafe just around the corner near the Exploding Forest of Doom."

The takeaway arrived and Matt ate three platefuls of macaroni cheese, and a carton of apple juice. Tom ate roast chicken and roast potatoes, sausages, and cucumber. He had chocolate ice cream and strawberries for pudding. Matt asked for raspberries, because he liked to stick them on his fingers like puppets.

Now that Tom was full up, he could think better.

"Jonny Supersonic," he said. "You said that Captain Chaos has an evil plan. What is it?"

Jonny stared at him. "I don't know! I thought you knew! You've been acting like his best friend! Didn't he tell you?"

The Chief of Police interrupted. "Captain Chaos wants to take over The Dog Star. Possibly Earth too. He plans to make **CHOCOLATE ILLEGAL**. So far we've always been able to stop him. But we've heard that he has a new, **SUPER SNEAKY** plan."

"Oh no," said Matt, and did a loud burp.

Normally, Tom would have laughed. But he had just remembered the worst thing.

"Jonny Supersonic!" he cried. "Captain Chaos has got our Mummy and Daddy!"

# 11.

# FART GUY

## TO THE RESCUE

*PARP!*

Tom jumped up. "We have to rescue Mummy and Daddy!"

Matt jumped up too. "We have to find the Cat Pan and put him in the bin!" he said. "Fart Guy to the Rescue! Pow!"

The Chief of Police shook his head so fast, all three of his chins wobbled. "You can't!" he said. "It's too dangerous! Captain Chaos is bananas! You don't know what he might do! Are these Mummy and Daddy people that important? I know...

Why don't I ask the prison doctor to delete part of your memory instead? That way, you will forget that Mummy and Daddy ever existed! It's marvellous what they can do these days!"

"No way!" said Tom. "We have to get Mummy and Daddy back. Come on, **JONNY SUPERSONIC**! We have to find them!"

Jonny Supersonic sighed. "If you insist," he said. "We'll take my ship. But! I warn you. Leave the fancy jumping about to me. I know what to do! If anyone can beat the Cat Pan, it's me!"

Tom grabbed Matt's hand and raised it to the sky. "**FIRE RAIDER** and **FART GUY** to the rescue!" he shouted.

LET the MISSION BEGIN!

# 12.
# TOM'S
# POWER

"Where are we going?" said Tom, as the spaceship shot off into the night.

"I have no idea," said Jonny Supersonic, fiddling with the controls. He had a funny look on his face.

Tom was a boy who always noticed if people looked happy or sad. This was a very special power. I think it was more special than being able to fly. But Tom didn't know that.

"What is it, Jonny Supersonic?" asked Tom. "Is something wrong?"

Jonny Supersonic looked a bit shy. Then he said, "I feel silly for asking."

"Never feel silly for asking!" said Matt.

## THE BADDIE

"Ok then," said Jonny. "What is a **DADDY**?"

Tom and Matt looked at each other and smiled.

"He gives me shoulder rides!" said Matt.

"He reads me bedtime stories!" said Tom.

"He makes us roast potatoes!" said Matt.

"He lets us watch television when Mummy says 'No'," said Tom.

"Wow," said Jonny Supersonic. "What is a **MUMMY**?"

"She is a beautiful princess," said Matt.

"She is a good driver," said Tom.

"She gives me hugs and kisses," said Matt.

"She can shout very loud," said Tom. "And then she told next door it was practise for a play."

"Mummy and Daddy love us," said Matt.

Jonny Supersonic looked sad. "We don't have Mummies and Daddies on the Planet Dog Star," he said.

"No Mummies and Daddies!" said Matt.

"Then how are you born?" said Tom.

"We are born from pods, like peas," said Jonny Supersonic.

"Oh," said Tom. How lonely that must be, he thought.

Then Matt said, "I want to watch a programme!"

If Matt was tired or sad, he always

liked to watch a programme or ten.

"You can't," said Tom. "We're in space!"

"Oh why?" said Matt in a whiny voice. "It's not fair!"

"Yes he can watch a programme!" said Jonny, quickly. "Here we go!"

Jonny Supersonic clicked his fingers, and a big TV screen whirred down from the ceiling.

"Cool!" said Matt.

"Can I watch my programme?" said Tom.

"Let him watch his programme first," said Jonny Supersonic.

"It's not fair," said Tom. "He always gets to do what he wants to do! I never get to do what I want to do!"

"Yes you do!"

"No I don't!"

"Stop it!" shouted Jonny. "If you fight, the Cat Pan will win! We have to be a team!"

There was a loud crackle from the TV.

The screen filled with fuzzy lines. And then a picture appeared of two green aliens shouting at each other, and one tall yellow alien in the middle, nodding.

Jonny changed channel. Another picture appeared of a lady in a red suit, talking.

"Not the news!" said Matt. "Boring!"

Jonny was about to press the remote, when Tom said, "Wait! Listen."

"Breaking news," said the lady, with a serious face. "More parents go missing. Martin Blabbermouth reports."

The picture cut to a man with big hair. He was standing over a little girl who was lying on the floor screeching and crying.

"Today, hundreds of children are being looked after by grumpy aunts and cross uncles, after their Mummies and Daddies vanished off the face of the earth.

"Questioned by police, it emerged that at least one hundred per cent of these children have admitted to biting a brother or sister, calling Mummy or Daddy 'an idiot', and refusing to eat a home-made dinner, calling it 'disgusting'.

"Have these little sirs and madams gone too far? Have these poor tired parents fled their tiny horrors and gone to sit on a desert island and read a nice book? Or could it be something more sinister?

"This is Martin Blabbermouth talking and talking. Back to the studio!"

Tom stared at the screen in horror.

"I know what the Captain's plan is!" he shouted. "We have to stop him before it's too late!"

# 13
# SILLY OLD DOGHEAD

Tom grabbed his light saver. "Captain Chaos wants all the Mummies and Daddies for himself!" he shouted. "And he is stealing them!"

Matt jumped up and down and pointed to the television screen. "It's the Cat Pan programme!" he said. "Silly old dog head!"

Jonny Supersonic and Tom stared. The Captain's face loomed over them. His eyes glowed purple.

"Well, well, Fire Raider," he sneered. "Aren't you clever? You can read peoples' minds!"

"No," said Tom. "I worked it out with my brain."

# THE BADDIE

"Who cares?" said the Captain. "You can't stop me! I've got your Mummy and Daddy! And you'll never find them! Now they are mine! Soon, no children will have Mummies or Daddies. All the Mummies and Daddies will work for me! They will make me eggs on toast! They will help me put on my socks! They will tuck me in all snuggly-wuggly at night! They will kiss me on the nose again and again! **HA HA HA**!"

The screen went blank.

Tom and Jonny Supersonic looked at each other in despair.

"Do something!" said Tom. "Use your powers!"

Jonny Supersonic shook his head. "My powers will only work if there is no other way."

"What does that mean?" shouted Tom.

"It means that if you can solve the problem with your powers, my powers freeze up."

"I don't have powers!" shouted Tom.

"Yes you do!" said Jonny Supersonic. "Or my powers would be working right now!"

Matt was looking out of a porthole at the millions of twinkling stars. "I see the moon and the moon sees me!" sang Matt.

Slowly, Tom stood up. "Yes!" he cried. "That's it, Matt! Well done!"

"Well there you go!" said Jonny Supersonic. "What a relief!"

Tom grinned. "The Cat Pan has taken the Mummies and Daddies to the Dark Side of the Moon! When we were in the spaceship with him, and you tried to gloop us, he said to retreat to the Dark Side of the Moon."

"Brilliant!" cried Jonny Supersonic. "He must have a secret lair! Oh no."

"What?" said Tom.

"It will take us three days to get there – which might be too late."

# THE BADDIE

"But can't you just burp us there?" said Tom. "You burped us from inside our house to your spaceship, remember?"

Jonny Supersonic sighed. "Yes. It's called a Displacement-Burp. You move the air, which then moves the object. But I can only do it once a year. It's too rude."

"I know, I know!" said Matt. And from out of his pants, he took a black felt tip pen. And he ran to the control panel and drew a black scribble. A **NEE-NAW BUTTON**.

"What is that?" said Jonny, crossly.

Tom smiled. "Press it, Matt," he said. "Show him."

**14.** THE DARK SIDE OF THE MOON.

There was a loud thud, and a cloud of silver dust blew up around the ship.

Jonny ran to a porthole.

They were in a large deep crater. The rocky walls of the crater were covered in pictures of the Captain. In every photo, he stood with his chest puffed out, his legs apart and his hands on his hips. He looked very pleased with himself and far more dashing than in real life.

"Amazing!" said Jonny Supersonic. "We must be inside the Cat Pan's lair, on the Dark Side of the Moon. Ok. Follow me."

NO.1 MOST GORGEOUS MAN

Jonny crept out. Matt and Tom crept behind him. Matt held the pasta scoop and Tom held the light saver.

"Watch out!" whispered Jonny Supersonic, pointing at the ground ahead. "That's a trap! We must go around it!"

Tom looked and saw a thin black net covering the rocky path. "Wait!" he said. "It could be a trick!"

"I don't mean to be rude," said Jonny Supersonic. "But I am older than you. I know what I'm doing."

Jonny Supersonic put his back to the rocky wall, and edged along it. He nodded to Tom and Matt to copy him.

Instantly, two big black hooks shot out of the wall and clicked together around Jonny's waist, like a huge pair of handcuffs.

Before Tom and Matt could jump to safety, they were also hooked.

"Fiddlesticks!" shouted Jonny Supersonic, kicking and flailing in mid-air.

In front of their eyes, silver lines began to

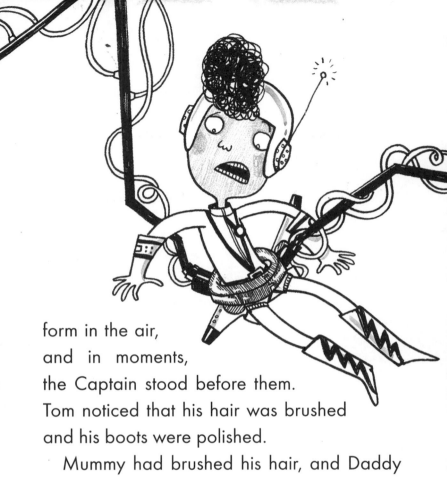

form in the air,
and in moments,
the Captain stood before them.
Tom noticed that his hair was brushed
and his boots were polished.

Mummy had brushed his hair, and Daddy
had polished his boots.

Tom wanted to cry.

"You nitwits!" said the Captain. "You can't
fool me! Now you are my prisoners!"

He laughed in a mean way.

"I want my Mummy," said Matt.

"Your Mummy is busy making me a cake!"
said the Captain.

"But Mummy can't make cakes! She buys them!" said Tom.

"Rubbish! All Mummies make cakes!" said the Captain.

Mummy's cake ↓

"I want my Daddy," said Matt. "Your Daddy is busy putting up pictures of me on the wall!" said the Captain.

"But Daddy can't do DIY. He just drills lots of holes!" said Tom.

**"QUIET!"** roared the Captain. He smiled. "Now, I'm having a story read to me, and then I'm going to have a nap, and then I am going to turn Mummy and Daddy into robots. That way, they'll last longer. Daddy has already complained of being tired," he said.

"Enjoy hanging out together! **HA HA HA**!" The Captain turned to go.

"I nearly forgot!" he said.

# THE BADDIE

And he snatched Jonny Supersonic's blasters out of his belt.

Then he vanished, and Tom, Matt, and Jonny Supersonic were left in the darkness.

## 15. HOOKED UP FOREVER

"Don't cry, Matt," said Tom. "Switch on your torch. Thank you." He smiled. "I bet these hooks are made of cardboard. I can easily rip them."

Tom peered down at the hooks, and his heart sank.

They were made of metal.

Matt shone his torch at Jonny Supersonic's hook. His was made of cardboard.

Oh no. The Captain must have worked it out. Metal was as soft as paper to aliens. And cardboard was as hard as metal to aliens. But for Earth people, it was the other way round.

"Can you do front flips and escape?" said

Tom, to Jonny Supersonic.

"Usually, but these hooks are just too tight," said Jonny.

"Can you do back flips and escape?" said Tom to Jonny Supersonic.

"Well... mm... not right now..." said Jonny.

"What about your supersonic punch that can punch through a wall?"

"The wall is behind me. It's a bit hard to punch something behind you."

Matt started to cry. "Now we are stuck here forever!"

# 16
## THE WONDER OF
## TEAMWORK

"No we're not!" said Jonny Supersonic. "Not if we help each other! I can rip your metal hooks, and you can rip my cardboard hooks!"

"Yes!" said Tom. "That's it!"

He tried to reach.

He couldn't.

"Here!" said Matt. "Use the pasta scoop!"

Matt passed the pasta scoop to Tom, who used it like a long claw. He got a hold on Jonny's hook and pulled hard. The cardboard tore and Jonny Supersonic jumped down.

"Yes!"

Jonny Supersonic grabbed the metal bars, which were trapping Matt and bent them apart.

# THE BADDIE

He lifted Matt down gently to the ground. Then he set Tom free as well.

"Yes!" they whispered.

This time, Jonny Supersonic let Matt and Tom lead the way. Slowly, quiet as mice, they tiptoed down the corridor. When they got to a corner, Tom peeped around it.

The Cat Pan was tucked up under a pirate duvet sucking his thumb and snoring loudly.

# TOM & MATT

There was Mummy doing a big pile of washing up with a cross face. Daddy was taking tea bags out of the sink and putting them in the bin, with an even crosser face. "Mummy! Daddy!" shouted Matt.

"Daddy! Mummy!" shouted Tom.

The Cat Pan woke up with a jump and reached for his blaster.

# SAVING
## 17. Mummy
### and
## Daddy

But Jonny Supersonic was faster – he was supersonic fast. He waggled his finger and 'splat!', the Captain was trapped in a big ball of green gloop.

"Fire Raider and Fart Guy have foiled your evil plan!" said Jonny Supersonic. "And the Chief of Police will be along shortly, to take you to jail. Pack an extra pair of pyjamas – you'll be there for a long time."

"Bother!" shouted the Captain and immediately swallowed a large amount of gloop.

# TOM & MATT

"Oh yes," said Jonny Supersonic. "And all the Mummies and Daddies will be returned to their children. They'll have a special jab, so they won't remember being kidnapped."

Matt tugged at Mummy's shirt. Mummy carried on washing up. "She's ignoring me!" wailed Matt.

"Jonny Supersonic!" said Tom. "Mummy and Daddy can't hear us! Maybe they are already robots!"

Jonny Supersonic ran over and checked Mummy and Daddy. "They're in the pre-stages. I can't change them back."

Tom and Matt gasped.

Jonny Supersonic smiled. "You can though," he said.

"How?" said Tom.

Jonny Supersonic

whispered in his ear.

Tom scrambled on to a chair, and kissed Mummy on the cheek.

"Darling!" she said. "My little prince!"

Jonny lifted Matt, who kissed Daddy on the cheek.

*Daddy in a daze*

"Hello, son!" said Daddy. "Aren't you cold wearing just pants?"

"Daddy, Daddy!" cried Matt. "This is Jonny Supersonic! He's a goody!"

Jonny Supersonic smiled. "We are all goodies," he said. "Now, who needs a lift home?"

Then Jonny Supersonic waved his silver glove. The movement left a trail of gold sparkles in the air. The sparkles grew, until each one was the size of a car. They were round with a spiky outside, like a conker in its case.

Jonny Supersonic waved his glove again, and the gold nuggets opened. They were little space capsules. Each one had a window, and inside was a soft chair and a lunch box. There was also a telephone, in case they wanted to call Mummy or Daddy.

"Step in!" said Jonny Supersonic.

Mummy, Daddy, Matt and Tom all climbed in to their space capsules.

Then Jonny Supersonic jumped into the air. The ceiling of the moon crater burst open and he flew through it, high into the sky. The four space capsules flew after him.

"**WOW!**" yelled Tom. "He's supersonic!"

"**WOW!**" yelled Matt. "He can fly!"

And Jonny Supersonic flew and flew,

with the four space capsules flying behind him like gold bubbles, until he got back to Earth. He flew so fast that Matt and Tom and Mummy and Daddy had just enough time to eat the chocolate sandwiches in their lunch boxes. Then they were home.

# 18. THE HEROES RETURN

The next morning, Tom and Matt woke in their beds at home. Daddy was whistling in the shower. Mummy was singing 'Don't You Forget About Me!', and the baby was banging a wooden spoon.

Tom and Matt ran downstairs. "Mummy!" shouted Tom and gave her a hug. Then Matt said, "Mummy, were you scared of the Cat Pan?"

"Who is the Cat Pan, darling?" said Mummy. "Is he from a programme?"

Matt gazed at Mummy. "You went to space, remember?"

## THE BADDIE

Mummy smiled. "Ah yes, we had a lovely game."

"We did, didn't we?" said Daddy trotting into the kitchen and swinging Matt into the air.

"They don't remember," whispered Tom to Matt.

And now, Tom was unsure. Had it been a game? There was no sign of Jonny Supersonic, and when he checked in the Hide Out, it was empty and he was not invisible. Mummy's pasta scoop was in the drawer, and his light saver and sword were in the toy box.

"Was it all pretend?" said Tom.

"Yes," said Matt, who was putting on lipstick.

"Go and play in the garden," said Mummy. "It's a lovely sunny day."

Gloomily, Tom plodded into the garden. Matt raced ahead to find a football.

# TOM & MATT

Tom gazed up at the blue sky. There was a faint wisp of moon.

"Tom!" shouted Matt from the end of the garden. "Come here! Look!"

Tom ran.

And there, parked in the middle of the flowerbed, with purple stripes painted on its sides and a green flashing control panel, was the captain's spaceship.

# THE END